The Surprise Party

Contents

Written by Susannah Reed

Illustrated by Andrea Castro Naranjo

Collins

What's in this story?

Listen and say

mirror

birthday cake

fancy dress costume

party

Download the audio at www.collins.co.uk/839658

phone

invitation

COME TO A FANCY DRESS PARTY

idea

It was Sunday. Amy was at her friend Grace's house.

"It's Polly's birthday on Saturday," said Amy. "I want to give her a surprise."

"It's your birthday, too," said Grace.

"Yes, I know," said Amy. "But my surprise is for Polly."

"Let's have a picnic on the beach," said Grace. "Polly loves swimming in the sea. And picnics are always fun."

"Hmm, yes," said Amy, "but it's winter now.
We can't have a picnic in the winter.
It's very cold."

"You're right," said Grace.

"I know. What about a game of football?" said Amy. "We've got eight friends — that's ten football players!"

"Hmm. I don't know," said Grace.
"We love football and Polly loves football, but not everyone enjoys football."

"You're right," said Amy.

"I know," said Grace. "Let's have a surprise party."

"What a great idea!" said Amy. "Everyone loves parties."

Surprise!

"Let's have a fancy dress party," said Amy.

"That's a good idea!" said Grace. "I can help you."

"Thanks, Grace," said Amy.

Chapter 2 Monday

On Monday, Amy and Grace made invitations for their friends. Amy drew the pictures and Grace wrote the words. The invitations looked beautiful.

They carried the invitations into town.
But then Amy fell and dropped them.
The invitations fell into the river.

Chapter 3 Tuesday

On Tuesday morning, Amy phoned
their friends.

"Can you come to a party on … ?"
she asked.

"Yes, of course," they said. "See you
on Saturday."

"That's funny," thought Amy.
"They all said, 'See you on Saturday.'
How do they know?"

Chapter 4 Wednesday

On Wednesday, Amy made a fancy dress costume. She found lots of old boxes.

"I can be a robot," she thought.

On Thursday, Amy showed her costume to Grace.

"You aren't a robot," Grace said, "but you're a good monster!"

Amy looked in the mirror. "You're right," she said.

Chapter 6 Friday

On Friday after school, Amy and Grace were in Amy's kitchen.

"What now?" asked Grace.

"Let's make a big, chocolate birthday cake!" said Amy. "Polly loves chocolate cake!"

Amy and Grace finished the cake.

"Hmm," said Grace. "Is it right?"

"Don't worry," said Amy. "Let's add more chocolate!"

Chapter 7 Saturday

It was Saturday. It was the day of the party. Amy's friends were at the door.

Amy and Polly both have a surprise party!

"Thank you, Polly," said Amy.

"Thank you, Amy," said Polly.

Picture dictionary

Listen and repeat

carry

drop

idea

mirror

monster

party

picnic

robot

winter

1 Look and order the story

Surprise!

2 Listen and say

Collins

Published by Collins
An imprint of HarperCollins*Publishers*
Westerhill Road
Bishopbriggs
Glasgow
G64 2QT

HarperCollins *Publishers*
Macken House,
39/40 Mayor Street Upper,
Dublin 1
D01 C9W8
Ireland

William Collins' dream of knowledge for all began with the publication of his first book in 1819.

A self-educated mill worker, he not only enriched millions of lives, but also founded a flourishing publishing house. Today, staying true to this spirit, Collins books are packed with inspiration, innovation and practical expertise. They place you at the centre of a world of possibility and give you exactly what you need to explore it.

10 9 8 7 6 5 4 3 2

ISBN 978-0-00-839658-9

Collins® and COBUILD® are registered trademarks of HarperCollins*Publishers* Limited

www.collins.co.uk/elt

British Library Cataloguing in Publication Data

A catalogue record for this publication is available from the British Library.

Author: Susannah Reed
Illustrator: Andrea Castro Naranjo (Beehive)
Series editor: Rebecca Adlard
Publishing manager: Lisa Todd
Product managers: Jennifer Hall and Caroline Green
In-house editor: Alma Puts Keren
Project manager: Emily Hooton
Editor: Frances Amrani
Proofreaders: Natalie Murray and Michael Lamb
Cover designer: Kevin Robbins
Typesetter: 2Hoots Publishing Services Ltd
Audio produced by id audio, London
Reading guide author: Emma Wilkinson
Production controller: Rachel Weaver
Printed and bound by: Pureprint, UK

MIX
Paper | Supporting responsible forestry
FSC
www.fsc.org
FSC™ C007454

This book contains FSC™ certified paper and other controlled sources to ensure responsible forest management.

For more information visit: www.harpercollins.co.uk/green

Download the audio for this book and a reading guide for parents and teachers at www.collins.co.uk/839658